FRIGHTMARES™

The
Ghost
Followed
Us Home

Peg Kehret

A
MINSTREL®
BOOK

PUBLISHED BY POCKET BOOKS

New York   London   Toronto   Sydney   Tokyo   Singapore

A MINSTREL PAPERBACK *Original*

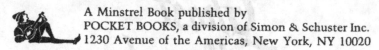

A Minstrel Book published by
POCKET BOOKS, a division of Simon & Schuster Inc.
1230 Avenue of the Americas, New York, NY 10020

ISBN: 978-1-4169-9110-6
ISBN: 1-416-99110-7
First Minstrel Books paperback printing January 1996

10 9 8 7 6 5 4 3 2 1

Cover art by Dan Burr

Printed in the U.S.A.

For Brett Konen

The Ghost Followed Us Home

CARE CLUB

We Care About Animals

I. Whereas we, the undersigned, care about our animal friends, we promise to groom them, play with them, and exercise them daily. We will do this for the following animals:

> **WEBSTER** (Rosie's cat)
> **BONE BREATH** (Rosie's dog)
> **HOMER** (Kayo's cat)
> **DIAMOND** (Kayo's cat)

II. Whereas we, the undersigned, care about the well-being of *all* creatures, we promise to do whatever we can to help homeless animals.

III. Care Club will hold official meetings every Thursday afternoon or whenever else there is important business. All Care Club projects will be for the good of the animals.

Signed:

Rosie Saunders

Kayo Benton

Prologue

Sedan, France
August 1914

Chantal Dubail ignored the distant gunfire.

"Sing for the soldiers," Chantal said as she pushed on the sides of her new musical cat. She worked the bellows in and out, in and out, smiling as the gray mohair cat produced a brief tune.

"Good Kitty," Chantal said. "Your music makes the soldiers happy. Papa and Jacques and all the other brave French soldiers clap when they hear your song." She lifted the cat to her face and kissed its velvet ears.

"Chantal!" Mama's cry startled Chantal out of her daydream. "Hurry! We must hide in the barn."

Chantal frowned, not wanting to leave her game. She was tired of hiding, tired of hearing guns in the distance. Tired of war.

She pulled her blue kerchief farther down over

her ears, trying to block out the sound of Mama's voice.

This time, she decided, she would not hide with Mama. She and Kitty would stay here and finish their pretend concert for the French soldiers. Mama could hide in the barn by herself.

It was Chantal's sixth birthday, after all. On her birthday she should be allowed to play with her gift. She should not have to hide from the German army.

The Germans never came, anyway. Three times already this week Chantal had left her games to hide in the barn, only to emerge hours later, tired and cross and smelling of cow manure, when the threatened attack failed to happen.

"Chantal!" Mama's voice was urgent now. "Hurry! The Germans are coming this way. I hear shots."

Chantal pressed herself against the floor beside her bed and squeezed her eyes shut, pretending to be asleep.

She heard Mama run into the room. Chantal lay still.

Mama grabbed Chantal's arm, jerking her to her feet.

"Come, Chantal," Mama said. "We must hide. Quickly!"

Chantal reached back to get Kitty, but Mama was already dragging her toward the door.

2

"Wait!" Chantal said. "I want to take Kitty."

"There is no time for toys," Mama said. "Run, Chantal! Run!"

Mama raced across the dirt yard to the barn, pulling Chantal with her. Tears puddled in Chantal's eyes, and she stumbled over a rock.

Inside the barn, Mama pointed to the stall where Sylvie the cow chewed her cud. "Get in the stall with Sylvie," she said. "Pull hay over yourself and lie very, very still. Stay quiet until I come for you."

The tears spilled down Chantal's cheeks. "I want Kitty."

"Do as I say, Chantal! Now!" Mama turned and climbed up the ladder to the hayloft.

Chantal ran into the cow stall and crouched in the corner, near Sylvie's head. She listened to the noises outside. They came from the direction of the river.

Rifle shots. Voices.

The shouting was louder than it had been on previous days. As she listened, the gunfire grew louder still. Closer.

Chantal lay down and pulled hay over herself. The dry hay made her skin itch and she scratched at her cheek.

Boom! Boom! Boom! A series of shots echoed across the barnyard.

Sylvie swished her tail and mooed.

3

FRIGHTMARES

A shudder ran down Chantal's arms. The German soldiers were really coming this time. The horrible German soldiers, the men Papa and Jacques had gone away to fight, were coming here, to her farm. The soldiers were marching across Papa's wheat field, trampling the grain.

What would they do to Chantal's house?

Before Papa and Jacques went away to fight, Chantal had heard them talk about how the German soldiers plundered the buildings in their path, looting and burning. Would they set fires here? Would Chantal's house soon be rubble and ashes?

Kitty! The German soldiers will burn my Kitty, Chantal thought. I must save her!

Chantal flung the hay aside and sprang to her feet. She ran to the door of the barn and lifted the heavy wooden latch. When the door swung open, she dashed across the yard toward the house.

"Kitty!" she cried. "I'm coming! I'll save you!"

A single shot rang out, sharp and loud.

"Kitty!"

Chapter

1

"This is terrible," Kayo Benton said as she brought the *Oakwood Daily Herald* newspaper inside. "Someone broke into the doll museum."

Kayo's best friend, Rosie Saunders, leaned over Kayo's shoulder and they read the article together.

DOLL MUSEUM BURGLARIZED

The Oakwood Doll Museum was broken into early this morning. The museum's burglar alarm went off at two A.M. When police arrived five minutes later, the thieves had left.

Police Chief Brian Stravinski said there were no clues to the identity of the burglars.

The door to a small office had been forced open and . . .

Kayo flung the newspaper down in disgust without finishing the article. "I am going to quit reading the news," she said. "It's too depressing to know what goes on in the world."

"That's why Mom does her U.K.s," Rosie said. "She says there are so many unexpected bad things that the rest of us have to do unexpected kindnesses, in order to balance it out."

"It will take a lot of U.K.s to make up for robbing the doll museum," Kayo said. "That's my favorite place in the whole world. Except for baseball fields, of course."

"Mine, too," Rosie said. "I hope the thief didn't steal the miniature dictionary."

"Or the Jackie Robinson doll," Kayo said. "That doll even has a tiny Ted Williams bat, and a little ball, and number twenty-four on his Dodger uniform."

"Remember the musical cat?" Rosie said.

"Oh, I hope the musical cat wasn't stolen. It was the best toy of all. Remember how we wished we could play it?"

Rosie nodded, remembering. The girls had gazed into the glass display case, admiring the gray mohair cat. With its black and yellow glass eyes, its embroidered toes, and its ears lined with

6

light gray velvet, the cat looked almost lifelike. It even had a tiny pink tongue.

Rosie had read the information card aloud. " 'Made in France, circa 1900.' "

"What does *circa* mean?" Kayo asked.

"I don't know," Rosie replied. "The information cards on some of the other dolls also say *circa* before the date. I think it means 'approximately,' but I'll look it up when I get home. We need a vocabulary word for this week."

Rosie took her notebook and pencil from her hip pocket and wrote *circa*.

Kayo read the rest of the information on the cat's card. "Mohair. Maker unknown. Internal bellows play music when cat is squeezed."

"What a wonderful toy," Rosie said. "It looks brand-new, as if nobody ever played with it."

"If I had a musical cat," Kayo said, "I would play it all the time."

Now, only three days after they had visited the doll museum, Rosie gave the newspaper a kick, crumpling the pages. "What kind of lowlife person would break into the doll museum?" she said. "Why couldn't they steal computers or television sets or jewelry? It's like robbing Santa Claus."

Kayo sighed. "Remember how everyone at the doll museum was smiling?"

Rosie nodded. "It's such a happy place. Mom

7

and Dad said they were reminded of their childhood."

"I don't suppose it's a happy place today," Kayo said.

"Let's go there," Rosie said. "I want to know if our favorite toys were taken or not."

"All right," Kayo agreed. "But if the burglar took the musical cat and the Jackie Robinson doll, I won't be able to stand it."

Half an hour later Kayo and Rosie got off the bus and, sharing Rosie's umbrella, hurried through a light drizzle toward the doll museum.

Just inside the front door a doughnut-shaped reception counter was equipped like a small office. The woman in the center, a volunteer docent, collected admissions, answered the phone, and directed visitors.

"We're sorry about the robbery," Kayo said as the girls paid their admission. "I hope the thief didn't get your musical cat."

"Nothing was stolen," the woman said. "The burglars broke into the office. We know they found the keys to the displays because the keys had been moved, but no dolls were taken. We think the police arrived before the theft could be carried out. Or else the thieves were looking only for money."

Behind the reception counter was a large open area. Two stairways, one against the right wall and one against the left, led to the second floor. A sign directed visitors up the stairs on the right; the other stairs were used to exit the second-floor exhibits.

Rosie and Kayo walked slowly through the entire museum. They watched three videos and learned that dolls have been made for thousands of years. Some were even made of bone.

They looked at a doll stove with copper pans, and a dollhouse equipped like a pet store. Another display showed an old-fashioned hospital with little nurse dolls, beds, carts, tables, and even a doll wheelchair.

"The beds and other equipment were salesmen's samples," Rosie said. Rosie always read the information cards.

They were in a special temporary exhibit of angel dolls when a loudspeaker announced that the museum would close in fifteen minutes.

Surprised, Rosie looked at her watch. "We've been here almost two hours."

"I want to go in the museum store before we leave," Kayo said.

They looked at the paper dolls, teddy bears, and books in the store until the closing announcement was made.

"You're the last to leave," the woman at the circular counter said as the girls headed for the door. "You must have enjoyed the museum."

"We did," Kayo said. "We always do." She opened the door. "It's raining again," she said. "Hard."

Rosie stopped. "My umbrella," she said. "I left my umbrella upstairs, in the rest room."

"Go get it," the woman said as she put on her coat. "But hurry, please. The museum is closed."

Rosie and Kayo hurried up the righthand stairway. The women's rest room was at the top of the stairs.

When Rosie tried to go in, the door was locked. "Someone is in there," she told Kayo.

"That's odd," Kayo said. "If we're the last to leave, who's in the rest room?"

"It must be one of the museum staff," Rosie said.

Kayo looked at the closest exhibit while they waited for the person in the rest room to come out. The lights on the second floor were turned out. The dolls looked different with only the light that came from the open stairway.

Rosie tried the door again, just to be sure. "Still locked," she said.

Kayo wandered toward an exhibit of large French dolls. She moved slowly in the dim light, her footsteps silent on the thick carpet. As she looked at the French dolls, she heard faint music.

She stood still and listened. It was a strange tune, played on an instrument she did not recognize. The same few notes were repeated, over and over, as if someone were practicing a brief passage in a song, trying to get it right.

Curious, Kayo moved through the dark rooms toward the music.

The odd tune continued as Kayo approached.

She stopped walking when she saw the source of the music. A chill slid down the back of her neck and tingled through her arms to her fingertips. Kayo swallowed hard and backed away.

Rosie still waited outside the locked bathroom.

"Come with me," Kayo whispered.

"What is it?" Rosie asked. "What's wrong?"

"Shh." Kayo put her finger to her lips and led Rosie through the dark museum.

Kayo could tell when Rosie heard the music, too. She suddenly stopped walking and looked around. Kayo steered her around the corner and past more displays, barely visible in the faint light.

It was the same tune as before, repeated over and over.

The girls moved toward the sound until they stood together, staring into a glass display case. The odd music came from inside the case.

"Look," Rosie whispered.

Kayo whispered back. "It's the musical cat."

Chapter

2

W atch the cat's back legs," Kayo said.

Rosie saw the legs of the mohair cat move rhythmically in and out as if hands were pressing and releasing them.

The odd music tinkled into the dark museum.

"How does that work?" Rosie whispered. "There aren't any wires. It isn't plugged in."

Kayo peered into the display case, her nose only an inch from the thick glass. "Maybe it's battery operated," she said.

"I don't think they had battery-operated toys in 1900," Rosie replied. "Besides, it says on the card that the cat plays music when the bellows inside it are squeezed."

"Someone's playing it," Kayo said.

"Someone invisible."

The Ghost Followed Us Home

The music stopped.

Thump.

Both girls jumped at the sudden noise.

Thump. Thump.

The girls looked at each other, their eyes wide with alarm. They looked at the display case again. No one was there, yet they could clearly hear the thumping noise, as if a person were inside the case, pounding against the glass.

Thump. Thump. Thump.

"Who's there?" Rosie said.

The pounding stopped.

"Girls?" The voice came from downstairs. "Are you coming?"

Rosie and Kayo ran back to the rest room. Rosie tried the door again. This time it opened. Her umbrella stood in the corner beside the sink, where she had left it.

She grabbed the umbrella and they hurried down the stairs. The woman stood by the door, waiting for them.

"Sorry it took so long," Rosie said. "The rest room was occupied, so we had to wait."

"We heard music upstairs," Kayo said.

The woman opened her mouth as if to say something and then closed it again.

"It came from a toy cat," Kayo continued, "but we couldn't see who was playing it."

The woman hesitated for a moment, as if deciding how to reply. "We pipe in music on a sound system," she said at last. "That must be what you heard."

Before Kayo could disagree, the woman opened the door and held it, indicating that Rosie and Kayo should leave. "Come back soon," she said. She smiled pleasantly, but the girls could tell she wanted them to go.

Rosie put up her umbrella, and the two girls stepped out into the downpour. The woman closed the door behind them.

"That was *not* piped-in music," Kayo said.

"She knew what it really was, but she didn't want to tell us."

Rosie and Kayo started toward the bus stop.

"What do you think that pounding noise was?" Kayo asked.

"It was hands, banging on the glass."

"Hands we couldn't see," Kayo said.

"It was a ghost," Rosie said.

The girls stopped walking, and looked at each other.

"A ghost was playing the musical cat," Rosie said, "and when it realized we were there, watching and listening, it quit playing with the cat and started banging on the glass. It probably wanted to frighten us away."

Kayo shivered. "I didn't know you believed in ghosts," she said.

"I never thought about them much until now, but how else can you explain what happened?"

"I can't," Kayo said. "Someone we could not see was pushing that cat's sides in and out. And it certainly sounded as if fists were banging on the glass."

"I think a ghost locked the bathroom door, too," Rosie said. "The door was locked and then unlocked from the inside, but nobody came out, and there was no one in there when I went in to get my umbrella. It had to be a ghost."

"Why would a ghost lock us out of the bathroom?"

"I don't know."

"I thought ghosts always haunted old buildings," Kayo said, "such as old churches next to graveyards or old houses where they used to live."

"The museum isn't very old," Rosie said.

"But the dolls are."

As they waited at the bus stop, Rosie felt uneasy. It was a vague discomfort, a sense that something was not right, although she didn't know exactly what.

It's the rainy weather, she told herself. The low clouds and fog brought early darkness, and a damp chill seeped beneath her sweatshirt. Rosie shivered.

The uneasy feeling grew stronger.

Rosie had felt this way in the airport once, when she was waiting for her uncle's plane to land. That time Rosie had realized someone was watching her. When she had looked around, she saw one of the teachers from her school. Rosie waved, the teacher waved back, and the uneasy feeling disappeared.

Now, as Rosie waited for the bus, she had that same feeling. *Someone is watching us,* she thought, but every time she turned around the sidewalk was empty.

"Why do you keep looking behind us?" Kayo asked.

"That business in the doll museum has me spooked, I guess."

"It doesn't make sense," Kayo said. "We heard fists pounding on the glass, as if a person were inside the display case, trying to get out. But if it was a ghost, it could just go in and out through the glass, couldn't it?"

"I don't know."

"I thought ghosts could go anywhere they want. In movies they float right through walls and windows and even locked doors."

"Not everything in movies is true," Rosie said. She glanced around again. The feeling was stronger now. Although she saw no one behind her, she was sure someone was watching her.

"Here comes our bus," Kayo said.

Rosie glanced around one more time. She gasped and pointed. "Look back there," she said. "By that tree."

Kayo turned and looked. "What? I don't see anything."

"A man. I saw a man in strange clothes. He's watching us." Rosie had barely glimpsed the man, but she had seen enough to know he was wearing some kind of costume.

"I don't see anyone," Kayo said.

"He must have ducked behind the tree."

The bus rumbled to a stop and the door creaked open. Kayo got on. As Kayo dropped her money in, Rosie paused with one foot on the step, looking back at the tree.

"There!" she cried. "I saw him again! There *is* a man watching us."

Chapter 3

Kayo bent to peer out the side window.

"Move to the back of the bus, please," the driver said.

Rosie stepped into the bus. Her hand shook as she released her coins.

Kayo slid into a seat by a window and looked toward the big tree. A faint blue light shone around the tree trunk.

Rosie sat behind Kayo, also by a window. She cupped her hands on the sides of her head, to see better, and stared at the empty sidewalk.

"I don't see the man," Kayo said, "but I see a funny light, as if somebody has a flashlight with a blue bulb in it."

"I don't see him now, either. He must be in back of the tree. That's where the light is coming from."

As the bus pulled away from the curb, Kayo moved back to sit beside Rosie.

"Are you sure the man was watching us?" Kayo asked.

"Positive."

"Maybe he lost something and was looking for it with a flashlight."

"No," Rosie said. "He was definitely watching us. I only got a glimpse, but he wore some kind of old-fashioned military costume, with a helmet."

"Weird," Kayo said.

"There was something very strange about that man."

"It's a good thing the bus was on time."

The girls rode along in silence for a few blocks, watching a young mother try to keep a toddler on the seat.

"I'm glad you're spending the night at my house," Kayo said. "Mom has a meeting tonight, and after what happened in the museum, and then that man watching us, I would not be thrilled to stay home alone."

The girls got off the bus at the corner nearest Kayo's apartment.

As soon as Rosie's feet touched the ground, she was engulfed by the same, strange feeling of uneasiness.

"Kayo," she whispered. "I think he followed us."

Kayo frowned. "How could he?" she said. "Wasn't he walking? You said he was behind a tree."

Rosie looked nervously in all directions, her anxiety growing.

"If he was on foot," Kayo said, "he couldn't possibly keep up with the bus. We only stopped a few times."

Rosie knew Kayo was right, yet she couldn't shake the feeling that she was being watched.

"All that craziness in the museum made you jumpy," Kayo said. She unlocked the door and put her foot carefully inside to keep Homer and Diamond from running out. When she had made sure the cats weren't lurking behind the door, trying to escape, she went in, and then held the door open for Rosie.

Rosie did not go in. She stood just outside the door, as if her shoes were glued to the steps.

"Are you coming?" Kayo said.

"I saw him again," Rosie said, her voice trembling. "He was right over there." She pointed toward the street.

Kayo stepped outside and shut the door. She surveyed the empty street. "I don't see anyone," she said.

"I don't see him now, either." Rosie frowned.

"But where would he go? There isn't any tree to hide behind this time."

"I know," Rosie said. "He just sort of— disappeared."

"Are you sure it was the same man?"

Rosie nodded. "Unless there are two people running around in an old uniform and a helmet, it was the same man I saw back at the bus stop."

Kayo looked both ways. She saw a young couple, their arms around each other, strolling down the sidewalk on the opposite side of the street. She saw the woman who lived in the apartment directly above Kayo, riding her bicycle home from the grocery store with a bag of groceries in the basket.

"There," Rosie whispered. "He's back."

Kayo looked where Rosie was pointing. "Oh!" she said. "I see him."

The man stood stiffly on the sidewalk, watching them. A faint blue light surrounded him.

He was tall, with a square jaw and large hands. He appeared to be in his mid-twenties, and he wore a dirty military uniform that looked as if it had been on him for weeks. The gray pants were tucked into knee-high leather boots, and he wore a helmet with a pointed ornament on top.

His blue-gray jacket had red piping and metal buttons on the front and sleeves. Shoulder straps were connected to a wide leather belt, from which hung four leather bullet containers.

"He isn't real," Kayo said, but before the words

were completely out of her mouth, the man vanished. One moment he was there and the next he was not, just like that.

Both girls remained still, staring at the spot where the man had stood. They waited, but he did not reappear.

Finally Kayo opened the door again, and this time Rosie followed her inside.

Kayo closed the door, locked it, and leaned her back against it. "Who do you think it was?" she asked.

"Who?" said Rosie. "Or what?"

"A ghost? Is that what you think?"

"He—it—disappeared into thin air," Rosie said. "What else can do that, besides a ghost?"

"I could see him," Kayo said, "but I could see behind him, at the same time."

Homer, Kayo's gray and white striped cat, came to greet them. Kayo leaned down to pet him as he rubbed against her ankles.

The doorbell rang. The girls glanced at each other in alarm.

Kayo looked through the peephole. "It's Sammy Hulenback," she said.

Rosie groaned. "Isn't he ever going to quit hanging around?"

Kayo opened the door.

"Are you having a meeting of your secret club?" Sammy asked.

"Yes," Kayo said. "And since it's secret, I can't invite you to come in." She started to shut the door.

"Wait!" Sammy cried, putting his foot inside the door to keep Kayo from closing it. "I have something to show you."

"Lucky us," Kayo said.

"What is it?" Rosie asked.

"It's an application to join your club." Sammy handed Kayo a piece of paper. "I want to track down thieves and catch vandals and chase after murderers, the way you do."

"That is not the purpose of our club," Rosie said.

"We'll consider your application and let you know," Kayo said. She closed the door.

"I've considered," Rosie said. "I vote no."

"I wouldn't let him in Care Club if he was a scout for the Yankees," Kayo said, "but we can't vote until we're having a meeting." She put Sammy's application on the small table beside the front door.

A low growl rumbled deep in Homer's throat. His fur stood straight out, making his tail seem three times its normal size.

"What's the matter with Homer?" Rosie said.

Kayo's orange cat, Diamond, stalked into the room. Her fur, too, stood on end, and her big amber eyes seemed focused on the same place where Homer was looking.

Homer hissed and swiped his paw across the air in front of him.

Kayo bent and tried to pick Homer up, but the cat backed away from her. "Nice Homer," Kayo said. "What are you growling at?"

"Kayo." Rosie's voice was little more than a squeak.

Kayo looked up.

The man in the uniform looked back at her. A faint blue light surrounded him. He stood in Kayo's front hallway, inside the door she had just locked.

"Who are you?" Kayo said. "What do you want?"

"*Komme*," the man replied.

"I beg your pardon?"

"*Komme schnell.*"

And then, before either girl could figure out what the man meant, he was gone again. A faint musty odor remained behind, the kind of smell that comes from a long-sealed box that's been stored in a damp basement.

Homer and Diamond sniffed the place where the man had stood, and then, their fur slowly returning to normal, they rubbed on Kayo's ankles, demanding their dinner.

"I can't believe what just happened," Kayo said.

"Neither can I. But it makes me nervous."

"It must be the ghost from the doll museum."

"Why would he follow us?"

"I don't know. But we never had a man appearing and disappearing before, not until we heard the musical cat and the pounding. It must be connected."

"The question is, what should we do about it?" Rosie said.

"There isn't much we can do about it, is there? If he came in here once, he can come in again, any time he wants to."

Chapter
4

"Did you understand what he said?" Rosie asked.

"No." Kayo shook cat food into two bowls. "It sounded like some other language."

"Maybe it wasn't a ghost. Maybe he's from another planet. Maybe a spaceship landed near the doll museum and we were the first Earth people he saw, so he followed us and he's trying to communicate."

Kayo put a bowl in front of each cat.

There was a knock at the door. Both girls jumped.

Kayo looked out the peephole.

"Is it him?" Rosie whispered.

"It's Sammy."

Kayo opened the door.

The Ghost Followed Us Home

"Am I in the club?" Sammy asked.

"We can't consider your application," Kayo said, "until we have an official meeting." She started to close the door.

"Wait a second," Rosie said. "Sammy, did you see anyone outside this building just now?"

"Yes," Sammy said.

"You did?" said Kayo.

"Was it a man in a military uniform?" said Rosie.

Sammy looked surprised. "No, it was your neighbor—the one who always rides her bike to the store."

"Oh," Kayo said.

Sammy leaned toward the girls, water dripping from his yellow rain slicker. "Who did you think I saw?" he asked. "Who was here wearing a military uniform? Is your secret club helping the army this time?"

"No," Rosie said.

"What's going on then? Why did you want to know if I saw a man in a uniform?"

"Forget it," Rosie said. "I made a mistake. It's nothing."

"We thought we saw someone we knew, but we were wrong," Kayo said.

"I don't believe you," Sammy said. "You're doing something exciting again, aren't you? And dangerous."

"I hope not," Kayo muttered as she closed the door.

After Mrs. Benton left for her meeting, Rosie said, "Let's have our Care Club meeting tonight. It will give us something to think about besides the ghost."

Kayo called the meeting to order and asked, "Is there any new business?"

"I met a woman in the pet store yesterday," Rosie said. "She helps find homes for greyhound dogs."

"Only greyhounds?" Kayo said. "Why not other dogs?"

"Greyhounds are bred for dog racing," Rosie said. "Lots of them aren't fast enough, and even those that are can only race for a few years. Some of the dog breeders don't bother to find homes for the dogs that can't race."

"What do they do with them?" Kayo asked.

"You don't want to know. The woman had a newspaper article that made me sick to my stomach."

Kayo gulped. "Oh," she said.

"Some breeders are unscrupulous," Rosie said, smiling because she had used a former vocabulary word. "The woman I met belongs to a Greyhound Rescue group. They go to Florida and Arizona and Idaho and other states that have dog

28

racing, and they take unwanted greyhounds and find good homes for them. Maybe Care Club can help."

"I can't adopt a greyhound. They're big and this apartment isn't."

"We don't have to adopt them ourselves," Rosie said. "We can do a report at school about the Greyhound Rescue efforts, or we can volunteer to help pass out their information, or we could raise money and donate it to them."

"Great idea," Kayo said. "I vote to help Greyhound Rescue."

"So do I. The phone number is at my house; we can call tomorrow and get started."

"There's one other piece of new business," Kayo said. "Sammy's Care Club application."

Rosie groaned, but Kayo went into the hallway, got the piece of paper, and brought it back to her bedroom. She unfolded it and began to read.

"Here is why you should let me join your Secret Club:
"1. I am smart and can help you figure out clues.
"2. I have a good bike so I can get over here fast whenever you need me to help chase criminals.
"3. I can keep a secret. I would not tell anyone about our Secret Club activities."

"It's signed, *Sammy Hulenback, Secret Agent Number Three.*"

"The trouble with this application," Rosie said, "is that Care Club is supposed to help animals, not solve crimes. Sammy wants to join because he thinks it will be exciting and dangerous, but I do not intend to get involved with any more criminals."

"Neither do I."

"Of course," Rosie added, "he also wants to join because he likes you."

"I move that Care Club reject this application," Kayo said.

"I second the motion," said Rosie.

"All in favor say aye."

"Aye," said Rosie.

"Aye," said Kayo. "The motion carries."

"The next time we see Sammy," Rosie said, "let's tell him that you have a boyfriend. If he thinks you like some other boy, maybe he'll quit hanging around."

"He'd want to know who it is," Kayo said.

"Tell him the boy lives out-of-town. He's a rock singer. Or a movie star. How about a boy from Texas whose family owns a bunch of oil wells?"

"The meeting," said Kayo, "is adjourned."

"Put in the minutes that we adjourned circa

cight o'clock," Rosie said. She took out her notebook and made a check mark on the page that said:

Circa: around or approximately. Usually used with dates.
Example: It was built circa 1889.

Rosie awoke in the night, aware that Homer lay across her feet. Kayo slumbered quietly in the other twin bed.

Rosie moved out from under the cat, and Homer quickly curled beside her again, purring softly. Smiling, Rosie reached down and stroked the thick fur.

She dozed then, half-asleep, half-awake. In this drifting dreamlike state, she smelled the same odd musty odor and realized the man was there. Even with her eyes closed she knew he stood erect in his rumpled uniform and his helmet, just inside the door. Sleepily she wondered who he was and why he was in Kayo's bedroom.

The smell intensified. Homer growled. A matching growl erupted from Diamond, who lay on the other bed next to Kayo.

The cats' warnings roused Rosie from her dreamy condition. She opened her eyes. The room was dark except for a glow of pale blue light around the man.

Rosie reached for her glasses and put them on.

31

She could see him clearly now—his uniform, his face, his eyes. She sat partway up, leaning on her elbows.

He gestured to her to follow him.

Rosie shook her head no.

As she gazed at the man, she knew he was not from this world. Although she could see the man, she also saw Kayo's closed bedroom door, which was directly behind him. She could look at the man and look right through him, at the same time.

She saw the buttons on his jacket, and the ornament on top of his helmet. She saw his pants, tucked into the tops of his high leather boots. At the same time she saw the doorknob and the poster of Willie Mays that Kayo had tacked to the back of her bedroom door. For an instant the drab gray-blue military uniform and the San Francisco Giants' uniform, with its black and orange lettering, blurred together.

Then the man took another step toward her and the blue glow intensified, blocking out the poster and everything else in the room.

Both cats leaped to their feet, with their fur extended and their backs humped up. Diamond hissed. Homer continued to growl.

Rosie reached across to the other bed and shook Kayo. "Wake up," she whispered.

"Umm," Kayo mumbled.

The Ghost Followed Us Home

Rosie shook harder, her own fear flowing from her hand into Kayo's shoulder. "Wake up!"

Kayo opened her eyes. "What?" she said.

"He's here," Rosie said. She heard the sharp intake of breath as Kayo saw the man, too.

Kayo sat up in bed, clutching the blanket tightly under her chin.

Curiosity mixed with horror as the girls watched the ghost.

Homer jumped to the floor and crept toward the ghost, his ears back and his body low.

The ghost held both hands out and beckoned to the girls to follow him.

"*Komme,*" he said.

"Go away," Kayo whispered. "Leave us alone."

The ghost's eyes shone with intensity, and he waved his hands toward them again. "*Komme so schnell wie möglich!*" he said.

Kayo reached for the bedside lamp and switched it on.

The instant the light came on, the ghost disappeared. Only a faint musty smell remained.

Chapter 5

Homer and Diamond sniffed the place where the ghost had stood.

Kayo got out of bed and walked to the closed door, avoiding the spot that the cats were examining.

She opened the door and looked into the dark hallway. "He's gone," she said and shut the door. "For now," she added.

Rosie took her notebook and pencil from the table on her side of the bed and began to write.

"This is not the time for vocabulary words," Kayo said.

"I'm trying to write what he said, so we can remember it." Rosie continued to write. "And I'm writing a description of his clothes. Maybe we can go to the library tomorrow and figure out where he's from and what he's trying to tell us."

The Ghost Followed Us Home

"Why would a ghost want to talk to us?" Kayo said. She moved nervously around the room as she spoke, taking shirts and jeans from the back of a chair and hanging them on hangers. "This whole thing gives me the creeps."

"He wants us to go somewhere with him," Rosie said.

"No way. I wouldn't go two feet with that—that—"

"Spook," Rosie said.

"Whatever he is, I wouldn't follow him if he offered me tickets to the World Series," Kayo declared. "Never! Never, never, never!"

"Shh," Rosie said. "You'll wake up your mom."

Kayo pulled a pair of sneakers from under a chair and put them in the closet. She wadded up a dirty sock, stretched her arms over her head, and pitched the sock into a hamper.

"Maybe he wants us to go back to the doll museum," Rosie said.

"What?" Kayo stopped cleaning the room and looked at Rosie.

"The doll museum is where all of this started," Rosie said. "He has to be connected somehow to the music and the thumping on the glass. I think he was in the museum, only we couldn't see him then, and now he's followed us home."

"I don't like it," Kayo said. "I don't want a ghost in my bedroom."

"Let's look up ghosts in your encyclopedia," Rosie said. "Maybe there's a way to get rid of him."

"Good idea." Kayo removed the G volume from the bookshelf and turned the pages until she came to the heading GHOST. She read aloud, "The spirit of a dead person, seen by the living."

Then she skimmed the rest of the material silently until she came to, "Although belief in ghosts is known in all parts of the world, their existence has never been proven."

Kayo handed the encyclopedia to Rosie. While Rosie read, Kayo went to her closet and got out her camera. "If he comes back," she said, "I'm going to take his picture."

"That would be proof," Rosie said. She looked at the words she had written. "Maybe he was speaking Italian. The words sounded Italian, don't you think?"

"I wouldn't know," Kayo said.

"Why would the ghost of a soldier be hanging around the doll museum?"

"Why is the ghost of a soldier hanging around us?"

"He wants to tell us something, or show us something." Rosie squeezed her eyes shut tight, the way she always did when she was trying to think. "Maybe the ghost saw the burglar," she said. "Maybe that's what he's trying to tell us." She opened her eyes. "The ghost saw the thief, and he knows there's some evidence at the museum that nobody has noticed and he wants to show it to us."

"Why us?" Kayo said. "We aren't F.B.I. agents. We aren't police detectives. We aren't even Girl Scouts. If a ghost knows who broke into the doll museum, he should let somebody from the museum know, not us."

"Perhaps they can't see him," Rosie said slowly, thinking it through as she spoke. "Maybe kids are more likely to see a ghost than adults are. I read one time about a three-year-old boy who talked about his friend, José. His mother thought it was cute that little Benjamin had an imaginary playmate and wondered where he had heard the name José, since the family knew no one by that name.

"One day Benjamin saw one of those Missing Child photos on a milk carton, and he pointed to the picture and said, 'There's José.' When his mother read the information, the missing boy's name was José."

"What did she do?" Kayo asked.

"Benjamin kept talking about his friend, and the games they played, so the mother called the

Missing Child hot line and asked if José was still missing."

"Was he? Was Benjamin really playing with José?"

"No. They said José's body had been found, three weeks earlier. He had drowned in the river."

"So the little kid was playing with a ghost," Kayo said.

"That's what the mother thinks. She never saw or heard José, but Benjamin played with him for a couple of months."

The girls were quiet for a moment, thinking of the little boy and his imaginary friend.

"My point," said Rosie, "is that kids are more open to unusual ideas, and so we saw the ghost, rather than an adult."

"Maybe some of the museum people see him and won't admit it," Kayo said. "The woman at the desk said the music we heard was their regular piped-in music, but I suspect she knew it wasn't."

"Exactly," Rosie said. "Maybe the ghost saw us admiring the dolls, and realized how much we like them, and thought we might be able—and willing—to help. So he tried appearing to us and now he knows we can see him."

"Every time he comes he stays longer," Kayo said.

"Or we see him longer every time. He might be here all the time but it takes practice for us to see him. You didn't see him at all at first, and I only had brief glimpses. But now that we've learned how, we see him more easily."

"I would just as soon quit practicing," Kayo said.

"We need to go back to the doll museum," Rosie said. "Tomorrow. We'll stay until it closes and then make up some excuse to go back upstairs. If the ghost is there, we'll find out what he wants."

"How?" Kayo said. "We won't be able to understand him any better tomorrow than we did tonight, so it won't do much good to follow him."

"At the museum he won't have to talk; he can show us what it is he wants us to see."

"It's worth a try," Kayo said. "I'll try just about anything if it will keep that spook out of my house."

Kayo got back in bed and turned out the light. The cats settled themselves again, but both girls lay staring into the dark.

"What are you thinking?" Rosie whispered.

"I wonder if we'll see him again tonight," Kayo said.

They did, just before dawn. The cats sensed his presence first, and their growling woke the girls.

FRIGHTMARES

This time the ghost didn't say anything. He didn't get a chance. As soon as Kayo woke up, she grabbed the camera from her bedside table, aimed it at him, and clicked the shutter.

The flash went off.

The ghost vanished.

Chapter 6

*T*he next afternoon Rosie and Kayo returned to the doll museum.

"I want to do this," Kayo said as they walked to the bus stop, "but I'm scared."

"So am I. I've never seen a ghost before. I don't know anyone who's ever seen a ghost. I like to read ghost stories, but I always thought they were made up."

"In the books I've read," Kayo said, "the ghost always wears a long, flowing white gown. I never heard of a ghost in a military uniform."

"He doesn't act as if he wants to hurt us," Rosie said. "He only wants us to follow him."

"Still, it's scary the way he suddenly appears out of nowhere, and I can't help wondering what will happen if he gets angry."

"If he appears at the museum, we will follow him," Rosie said. "Since that's what he wants, there would be no reason for him to get angry."

"What if something goes wrong? What if we get in major-league trouble and no one hears us call for help?"

"We won't leave the doll museum. What could go wrong there?"

"If we don't find out what the ghost wants," Kayo said, "he may keep appearing in my room at night. That idea is more scary than following him."

While they waited for the bus, Sammy rode up on his bicycle.

"Where are you going?" Sammy asked.

"To the doll museum," Kayo said.

Sammy wrinkled his nose, as if something smelled bad. "You don't still like dolls, do you?"

"As a matter of fact, we do," Rosie said.

"Dolls are for babies," Sammy said.

"Strike one," said Kayo.

"I thought you wanted to be a professional baseball player," Sammy said.

"I do," Kayo replied.

"Baseball players don't have anything to do with dolls," Sammy said.

"Strike two," Kayo said. "The doll museum even has a Jackie Robinson doll."

"Who?"

"You don't know who Jackie Robinson was?"

Kayo said. "I don't believe it." She removed her Chicago Cubs cap, pushed her long blond hair away from her face, and put the cap back on. "Jackie Robinson," she said, "was the first black player to play on a major-league team. He put up with insults and racial slurs, but he was Rookie of the Year and the National League's Most Valuable Player. He was the first black person to be inducted into the Baseball Hall of Fame."

Kayo planted both hands on her hips and glared at Sammy. "Until Jackie Robinson came along," she said, "only white men could play in the major leagues. He was a hero! How can you not know who Jackie Robinson was?"

"He knows now," Rosie said.

"I wouldn't go to a stupid doll museum if you paid me," said Sammy.

"Strike three," said Kayo.

"Nobody asked you to come," said Rosie.

Sammy said, "Tell me the truth. Where are you *really* going?"

"We told you," Kayo said. "We're going to the doll museum."

Sammy folded his arms across his chest and gave them a suspicious look. "It has something to do with the army, doesn't it? You guys are too smart to go look at a bunch of sissy dolls in a dusty old museum. You're going somewhere to meet the man in the military uniform."

"He's on to us, Kayo," Rosie said. "We may as well tell him the truth."

"Go ahead," Kayo said.

Rosie leaned toward Sammy and whispered, "We're going to the hospital. Some genetic scientists are doing secret experiments on human intelligence, and they asked us to participate. They want to know why we are so smart."

"We're going to have an operation," Kayo said.

Sammy gulped. "Both of you?"

"Yes," Kayo said. "On our big toes."

"Huh?"

"The theory," said Rosie, "is that the most highly intelligent people do not get their reasoning power from their brains, as everyone thinks. It comes from their big toes."

Sammy looked down at his feet.

A large green bus wheezed to a stop.

"Here's our bus," Kayo said.

"When will you get home?" Sammy asked.

"Circa midnight." Rosie made a check mark in her notebook.

The girls climbed on the bus and dropped their money in the coin receptacle.

"Typical Sammy," said Rosie as they found seats toward the back. "He's never been to the doll museum, but he thinks he knows all about it."

"If he knew how beautiful and valuable the

old dolls are, or what a gorgeous big building the museum is, he'd change his mind."

"What mind?" Rosie said. "That boy needs a new brain."

Kayo grinned. "Or a new big toe," she said.

They arrived at the doll museum at four. A different volunteer docent greeted them.

Upstairs, many people viewed the displays, admiring the beautiful dolls. Rosie and Kayo moved quickly from exhibit to exhibit.

"I'm too nervous to enjoy this," Kayo said. "I feel the way I did before I pitched in the league championship game." She raised both hands over her head, stretched, and threw an imaginary baseball.

"Maybe that's a good omen. That's when you pitched your perfect game." Rosie looked at her watch. "Four-thirty," she said. "I wonder if the ghost knows we're here."

By four forty-five, Rosie and Kayo were the only people remaining on the second floor. They waited by the musical cat.

"We're here," Rosie whispered. "You can come any time."

"The sooner, the better," Kayo added.

"Maybe he's here," Rosie said, "but we can't see him because the lights are too bright."

"He had better come as soon as the museum

closes. We'll have only a couple of minutes after five to find out what he wants. Then we'll have to leave."

"What if he doesn't come?" Rosie said.

"Then we'll know he didn't have anything to do with the doll museum, after all. We guessed wrong."

At one minute to five Rosie went downstairs. As she approached the desk, a group of women came chattering out of the museum store, headed toward the exit.

"My friend is in the bathroom," Rosie told the woman at the desk. "I'm going to wait for her; we'll be down soon."

The woman nodded agreement as she waved goodbye to the group of women and, at the same time, answered her telephone.

As Rosie rushed back up the stairs, the second-floor lights went out. She waited a minute at the top of the stairs, letting her eyes get used to the dark, before she walked through the exhibit rooms to where Kayo waited.

"Anything?" Rosie whispered.

"No."

The girls stood still, watching for the ghost in the uniform.

While they waited upstairs, the woman at the desk downstairs hung up the telephone, snatched her purse from a shelf, and let herself out of the circular reception area.

She rushed into a small office. "Would you lock up for me, please?" she said. "My neighbor called; her mother had a heart attack and she needs me to watch her baby while she goes to the hospital."

The woman dashed out the door and down the steps to her car. She was nearly home before she realized she had forgotten to say there were two girls still upstairs. No harm done, she decided. The girls would have come down long before anyone locked the doors. They would be on their way home by now.

But Rosie and Kayo were not on their way home. At five-fifteen, as the locks clicked into place downstairs and the burglar alarm was activated, the girls stood in the dark on the second floor of the doll museum, staring in disbelief into the display case which held the musical cat.

The ghost in the uniform did not appear.

A different ghost did.

Chapter 7

*I*t began with the music.

The brief tune played over and over, just as it had the day before. This time Rosie and Kayo recognized the sound of the musical cat and were not surprised to see its sides moving in and out as an unseen being pushed on it.

When the music stopped they waited, expecting to see the ghost who had followed them home. Instead, they saw the ghost of a small girl, not more than five or six years old.

She wore an ankle-length cotton dress, with a long white apron over it. A blue kerchief, folded in a triangular shape, was tied at the back of her neck, beneath her brown hair. Her face and hands were pale, and her whole body, including her clothing, was transparent.

"It's another ghost," Kayo whispered.

Rosie nodded. The ghost of a small girl was not as scary as the ghost of a large man in uniform. The child would have been appealing, except for one thing: Her face was contorted with grief. Sobs racked her small body and tears streaked her sorrowful face as she knelt inside the display case, pounding her fists against the glass.

Thump. Thump. Thump.

It was the same sound as before except this time Rosie and Kayo could see who was pounding. The ghost girl wept and banged frantically at the glass.

"Is she trapped in there?" Kayo asked as chills rippled down her arms.

Rosie did not answer. She had never seen anyone look as unhappy as the ghost girl looked.

The little girl did not appear to see them. Although her face was only a few inches from the inside of the glass, and Rosie and Kayo were only a foot from the outside, the ghost girl seemed to look right through them, without noticing that they were there.

Thump. Thump. Thump.

Rosie raised her own fist, hesitated a second, and then beat on the outside of the case. The thick glass vibrated.

The ghost, clearly startled, stopped pounding and blinked at them. She stared for an instant, the tears still rolling down her pale cheeks. Her hands reached through the glass toward Rosie and Kayo, as if she were begging for help. *"Petit chat,"* she said.

And then she vanished.

Rosie and Kayo pressed their faces to the glass but saw no more sign of the unhappy child.

A deep voice directly behind them said, "I think you do not speak French. Or German."

Rosie jumped. Kayo gasped. Both girls spun around to see who was there.

A blue glow lit the room, making all the dolls look as if they wore pale blue clothing and had blue skin. The same musty smell that had been in Kayo's bedroom filled the air.

The ghost in the uniform said, "You came. That is good." He spoke haltingly, with an accent; the girls had to listen hard to understand him. "And you know this language?"

"Yes," Kayo said. "We speak English."

"Good. I have not spoken for many years. It was difficult to know which Earth language to use."

"Who are you?" Rosie asked.

"I am Werner von Moltz." He saluted.

"Nice to meet you," Kayo said. "I think."

He pointed into the display case. "I did not mean to do it," he said.

"Do what?" Kayo said.

"I saw a sudden movement and thought the French were attacking me. I fired before I knew it was a child. In a war one does not wait for the enemy to fire first."

Rosie's voice was barely a whisper. "You killed her?"

He winced at the question. "I did."

"When?" Kayo asked.

"The war had just begun. We thought it would be over quickly and Germany would be victorious."

"Which war?" Rosie said.

"We called it The Great War, but I learned there is nothing great about war except the suffering. So many dead. So many wounded. And for what? What was gained? What was learned?"

"I don't know," Kayo said.

"The Great War," said Rosie, "was World War I."

"*Ach!*" Werner von Moltz slapped his palm to his forehead. "So many wars they must be numbered, to keep them straight."

Rosie glanced over her shoulder, wondering if the other ghost had returned, but she had not.

"After The Great War," Werner von Moltz said, "our noble leaders returned to their high offices and thought of new reasons to fight. They learned nothing, and I died knowing I had killed an innocent child."

"It was an accident," Kayo said. "You didn't mean to shoot her."

"Thank you," he said. He bowed slightly. "Thank you for believing that."

Werner von Moltz stepped close to the display case and looked in. "For all these years," he said, "I have tried to bring peace to Chantal's spirit, to make up for robbing her of her life. But I cannot make her happy. The only thing that will erase her sorrow is the return of her toy." He pointed into the display case.

"The musical cat?" Rosie said.

"Yes. She weeps for her kitty. She cried for it as she died, and she will grieve through all eternity if I do not find a way to help her."

"How terrible," Kayo said.

"I left my own body a few hours after Chantal left hers," Werner continued.

Rosie and Kayo glanced at each other, horrified, and then looked at the ghost again.

"I saw the child's sorrow and vowed to help her. When the fighting moved on, we went together, Chantal and I, to her home, but her kitty was not there. Perhaps it was hidden in a soldier's knapsack, a gift for some other child at war's end. I had no way to know who had it, or where.

"I searched for decades, roaming through all continents, to find this toy. I found it and brought Chantal here, but it is not within my power to dry her tears. I am unable to remove the kitty from its place."

"You came in my house through the locked door," Kayo said.

"Chantal and I can go anywhere because we are not of the Earth anymore. But her toy cat is physical, and I have no way to move it past the locked glass."

"If she can go in there she can play with the cat any time she wants," Rosie said. "Why is she still so unhappy?"

"She longs to be on French soil, just as I wish to return to Germany. Chantal needs to be near her home and near the graves of her parents. She wants her kitty there with her, in France."

"She was speaking French, wasn't she?" Rosie said.

"Yes. Chantal's language is French. Like her heart."

"Were you speaking German last night?" Rosie said.

"Yes. I asked you to come, as quickly as possible." He smiled at them. "And here you are."

"Why did you follow us?" Kayo said.

"I have followed many others since I found Chantal's toy. Only you acknowledged my presence. The rest do not see me or pretend not to see me. Or they are too frightened to listen."

"We can't help you," Rosie said. "We don't have a key to unlock the display case."

"*Ach!* I feared as much."

"We could talk to the people who work here," Kayo said. "If we tell them what you just said, maybe they would agree to open the display case."

"The musical cat is probably worth a lot of money," Rosie said. "The museum people may not want it to leave."

"Chantal will need her kitty only a short time," Werner von Moltz said. "If she can take it home to France, and play with it there, her tears will be gone, forever. And her unhappy spirit will be at peace. Forever. When that happens Chantal will no longer appear as a ghost. She will no longer care about Earthly toys."

"But the cat will be somewhere in France," Kayo said.

"I will try to return it," Werner said. An expression of great longing came over his face. "If Chantal's spirit finds peace," he said, "that will allow me to find peace, also."

"So you wouldn't appear as a ghost anymore, either?" Rosie said.

"That is correct. But I will try, before that happens, to return the musical cat."

Rosie turned to Kayo. "I think we should help him," she said.

"So do I," Kayo replied.

"You will speak to them?" Werner asked. "You will try to help me?"

"Yes," Kayo said. "We will try to help you."

"We'll do all we can," Rosie said.

"I thank you." Werner von Moltz saluted again, clicking his heels together sharply. The blue glow grew brighter and then he was gone, leaving Kayo and Rosie blinking into the darkness. Only a trace of musty odor remained.

"No one is going to believe this," Kayo said.

"We promised we'd try."

"I want to try," Kayo said. "That little girl was shot accidentally because she happened to live where a war was being fought. It seems only fair for her ghost to have her toy cat, if that is what she needs to be happy for all eternity."

"Last night," Rosie said, "I was afraid of the ghost, but now that we know what he wants, I'm not scared anymore."

"The woman at the desk is probably wondering what's taking us so long. Let's go tell her what happened and ask if she has keys. Maybe she would open the case right now."

They started toward the stairway.

"It's awfully dark in here," Rosie said. As soon as she said it, she realized why. While they were talking to the ghost, the lights from the first floor and stairs, which earlier had spilled onto the second floor, had been turned off.

Kayo said, "I hope she didn't forget we are here."

They walked carefully down the dark stairs until they reached the landing. From there they could see the main floor, with the circular reception counter. The lights were out throughout the entire museum. The only light filtered through the front windows, from the museum's outdoor lighting. Even the skylight looked shadowy.

"Everyone's gone," Kayo said. "It's already dark out."

Rosie pushed the button that illuminated the dial on her wristwatch. "It's after five-thirty," she said. "We missed our bus."

"I didn't know it was that late. We talked to the ghost a long time."

"My parents don't let me ride the bus after dark unless they're with me," Rosie said. "We'll have to call home."

"I'll call Mom," Kayo said. "She should be home from work by now."

"If she isn't we can call my dad. And we had better look for a night number for the museum. We can probably unlock the door and get out, but we wouldn't be able to lock it again. We can't go off and leave the doll museum unlocked. And what if we set off the burglar alarm?"

The Ghost Followed Us Home

They started down the second half of the stairs, moving slowly in the dark so they wouldn't fall. They were nearly to the bottom when they heard a creaking noise, ahead and to their right.

Both girls froze.

Another ghost?

Chapter

The girls crouched close to the side of the staircase.

Rosie's mind raced. It can't be the janitor, she thought. An employee would turn on the lights. And the two ghosts had moved silently. Except for his conversation Werner von Moltz made no sound.

Someone else was in the museum.

The creaking grew louder. It sounded like a wheel, as if a rusty wagon was being pulled toward them.

Kayo nudged Rosie with her elbow as two people entered the main room from the direction of the museum store. Both wore black clothing, including gloves. They had black ski masks over their heads, with cutouts for their eyes, noses, and mouths.

One of them pulled a low four-wheeled cart with a flat surface. Kayo had seen similar carts at a discount grocery store, except this one was piled with dolls.

The two people in black pulled the cart toward the bottom of the second stairway, the one visitors used to exit the second-floor displays.

"I hope these keys fit the second-floor displays," one of them said. It was a woman's voice. "We made the keys in a terrible hurry."

"We got in, didn't we? The key turned off the alarm. You got in the museum store and got the dolls you wanted." The second voice belonged to a man. "Why would the upstairs displays be any different?"

The man walked away from the cart. He stood between the museum door and the circular counter, looking outside. The woman started up the exit stairs.

"Make it fast," he said.

She paused. "I would be a lot faster," she said, "if you had thought to measure the elevator to be sure the cart would fit."

"The exercise will be good for you," he said.

"If climbing up and down stairs is so great, why don't you come and help?"

"I'll keep watch while you open the cases and get out the dolls you want. Then I'll come and

59

help you carry them. The first rule of successful burglary is 'Always post a lookout.'"

The woman climbed the other stairs and went out of Rosie and Kayo's view.

Moving together as if they were doing a choreographed dance, Rosie and Kayo slowly stood and backed up the stairs, keeping their eyes on the man.

They did not realize when they reached the landing. Rosie backed into the child-size oak piano that stood on the landing, and the piano slid across the floor, making a scraping sound.

The man turned.

Rosie and Kayo stood still on the dark landing, hardly daring to breathe. They could see him because he was next to the glass door, where the outside lights shined in.

"Was that you, Darlene?" he called.

"Yes," a voice replied from the second floor. "Come and help me carry these dolls."

The man loped up the stairs, returning shortly with his arms full of dolls. He dumped them on the cart.

"Be careful with those," the woman snapped as she, too, came down with an armload of dolls. "Break off one little pinkie and the price plummets."

"Only a crazy person would pay one hundred thousand dollars for a bunch of dolls," the man said.

"Mrs. Tuttle is not crazy. She's a shrewd businesswoman who will triple her money on these dolls." As she spoke the woman carefully laid the dolls she carried on the cart and then straightened the ones the man had dumped.

"Triple her money? You mean she's going to make more than we do on this deal?"

"We're making plenty."

"We should make the most. We're taking all the risks. My ears are still ringing from that burglar alarm shrieking the night we came in here to copy the keys."

"It was loud, all right."

"Tuttle's at home eating dinner right now while we take a chance on prison terms."

"Mrs. Tuttle has the contacts. She'll sell these to collectors in other countries, who have no idea they are stolen. What would we do with them? Do you have any pals who will pay big bucks for a Shirley Temple doll?"

The woman stomped back up the stairs. The man returned to his lookout post.

Rosie edged carefully past the small piano, and the girls crossed the landing. They started up the second half of the stairs.

Part way up, when they could no longer see the man, Rosie put her hand on Kayo's arm, indicating she should stop. She whispered in Kayo's ear, "I have an idea."

61

Kayo waited, growing more nervous by the second.

"I'll go back down," Rosie whispered, "to where we were when they first came. You wait on the landing. When he goes upstairs to help her carry the next load, you run to the second floor, make a big racket, and then lock yourself in the bathroom."

Kayo shook her head, no, but Rosie continued to whisper. "They'll go up to see what the noise is, and I'll dash to the telephone and call the police. The thieves will get caught in the act."

"What if they see you?" Kayo said.

"If they see me I'll run up the stairs and you can let me in the bathroom with you."

"Maybe we should both hide in the bathroom until they leave, and then call the police," Kayo said.

"We can't give descriptions of them or of their car," Rosie said. "They would get away. They would get all the dolls."

Kayo thought about Rosie's plan. "You should be the one to distract them and hide in the bathroom," she said, "and I'll make the call. I can run a lot faster than you. If they chase me I can probably get away; they might catch you."

Rosie knew Kayo was right. Kayo ran two miles every day as part of her training to be a professional baseball player. Rosie ran only when she was required to do so in P.E., and then she always finished last in the sixth grade.

Kayo sat and bumped down the stairs on her bottom. She scooted across the landing and then slid silently down the rest of the steps, pausing at each step to be sure the thief had not turned around.

The man stood as before, with his back to both stairways, looking out the front door.

Rosie crouched on the dark landing, careful not to touch the little piano. She also watched the man.

When Kayo's feet reached the main floor, she stayed seated on the second step up. Her hands pressed on the step and she leaned slightly forward, ready to spring up and run when it was time.

"Come and get them!" the woman called.

The man looked out the door in both directions, and then started toward the exit stairs.

As soon as he moved, Rosie ran. When she reached the second floor she let out a bloodcurdling scream, the kind she had heard in an old monster movie. Her voice echoed through the empty museum.

The man swore and began climbing up the stairs two at a time.

When he reached the landing Kayo shot to her feet and ran toward the circular reception area.

She had seen the telephone earlier, behind the counter.

She fumbled for the doorknob to open the waist-high door that led inside the area.

The door was locked. Kayo reached over and tried it from the inside, but the door did not open. It must need a key, Kayo thought. She put her hands on the marble counter and jumped, swinging her legs up.

Rosie screamed again.

The man stopped part way up the steps and looked behind him. As soon as he turned, he saw Kayo. Instead of continuing up, he ran back down.

Intent on climbing over the counter, Kayo took her eyes off the man and did not realize he had changed directions. She swung her feet inside the counter area and slid to the floor.

When she looked up the man in black was only a few feet away, rushing straight toward her.

Kayo knew instantly that she could not get away. He was too close. If she had been outside the circular reception area, she could have run, as planned, and joined Rosie in the bathroom.

But there was not time now to climb back over the counter and run. He would catch her easily.

Instead of running she searched for the telephone. Her fingers felt frantically along the ledge beneath the counter, where she had seen the woman pick up the telephone earlier.

The man put his hands on the counter and vaulted over the door. Kayo moved away from him as she continued to hunt for the telephone.

There! She found it. She raised the receiver as his feet hit the floor inside the reception area.

Kayo put her face close to the telephone, trying to read the numbers. She punched number nine.

The man lunged. Before Kayo could hit number one, his fist swung out, knocking the telephone from her hand.

Chapter 9

The telephone receiver clattered over the ledge and dangled toward the floor.

Kayo edged sideways away from the man, her back pressed against the rib-high counter.

Upstairs, the screaming stopped.

"Dutch!" the woman's shrill voice cried. "Come up! There's somebody in here."

The man did not answer her. He stepped closer to Kayo. "What are you doing in here?" he said. He spoke as if he owned the museum and Kayo had no right to be trespassing.

"I have permission to be here," she said. "I'm doing research on ghosts."

"Sure you are," the man said, "and I'm the President of the United States."

The Ghost Followed Us Home

The woman upstairs yelled again. "Dutch! Do you hear me? Someone is up here. He's locked himself in the bathroom."

"How did you get in?" the man asked Kayo. "Did you see me unlock the side door and turn off the burglar alarm? Or did you and your buddy come in during regular hours and hide somewhere until everyone left?"

"There's no one with me," Kayo said. "I came alone."

A nasal-sounding voice spoke from the floor near Kayo's feet. Kayo jumped.

The man's head jerked as he looked down.

The voice said, "If you'd like to make a call, please hang up and try again. If you need help, hang up and then dial your operator."

I would love to dial the operator, Kayo thought. I would trade my Johnny Bench rookie card for a chance to dial the operator.

"If you'd like to make a call," the voice repeated, "please hang up and try again. If you need help, hang up and then dial your operator."

"Be quiet," the man said, kicking at the telephone.

"There's no one in the bathroom," Kayo said. "That screaming you heard was one of the ghosts. They like to lock the bathroom doors as a joke. They do it all the time."

"There are no ghosts."

Beep beep beep beep beep. The telephone emitted a series of sharp sounds designed to attract attention. The man reached down, grabbed the receiver, and replaced it in its cradle.

Taking advantage of his momentary distraction, Kayo leaped up on the counter. She slid across it and dropped to the other side. When her feet hit the marble floor, she ran for the front door. It was much closer than the stairs. If she could make it out of the museum, she was sure she could run faster than the man. She would get to a telephone and call for help.

She knew Rosie would be safe in the bathroom. The thieves had keys to the museum and the display cases, but they would not have a way to unlock the bathroom door when it was locked from the inside.

The man jumped over the counter and started after Kayo.

Kayo stretched out her arm as she neared the door. She was almost there.

As Kayo's hand closed around the door handle, the man caught her. His hands clamped down on her shoulders and spun her around to face him.

The woman ran down the stairway. "Can't you hear me?" she said. "There's a person upstairs. Maybe more than one." She stopped running when she saw Kayo. "Who's that?" she asked. "How did she get in?"

Kayo stood with her back to the door, facing the thieves. Light from the museum's outdoor lights shone dimly in on their black clothing. Their eyes glittered angrily through the openings in the ski masks.

"She says she's here doing research on ghosts," the man said.

The woman stiffened. "Ghosts?" she said. "There arc ghosts in here?"

"Yes," Kayo said, sensing the woman's anxiety. "Lots of ghosts. The museum is haunted."

"My grandmother claimed she once saw the ghost of her father," the woman said. "Grandmother was only ten at the time, but she talked about it for the rest of her life."

"Are we going to stand around and swap stories about our dear old grannies," the man said, "or are we going to get those dolls?"

"There's a person upstairs in the women's bathroom," the woman said. "I heard terrible screaming, and when I went to investigate, I heard the bathroom door close and lock. Someone is in there."

"It's one of the ghosts," Kayo said. "The screaming was a ghost, too."

Maybe I can scare them off, Kayo thought.

Maybe I can make her so nervous she leaves, and he would go with her.

"The ghosts scream when they're angry," Kayo continued. "They don't like it that you're taking the dolls away."

As Kayo spoke the woman kept rubbing her hands together and looking over her shoulders.

The man said, "Don't give us any more ghost foolishness. We know better." He turned to the woman. "She probably has a friend with her," he said "and the other kid screamed."

"I thought there was a person upstairs," the woman said, "but I didn't actually see anyone. I heard the screams and then I heard the door click shut, and when I tried to open it, it was locked from the inside. Maybe it is a ghost, Dutch. Maybe this place *is* haunted."

"And maybe I'm going to win an Olympic medal in figure skating."

I wish the ghost would appear, Kayo thought. If the ghost of the German soldier materialized right now, this woman would faint for sure.

"If you take the dolls," Kayo said, "the ghosts will follow you."

"I don't like this, Dutch," the woman whispered. "Let's take what we have and get out of here."

"And let her call the cops before we get it

loaded in the van?" the man said. "No way. We are not leaving without everything we came for."

"My friend and I were here yesterday," Kayo said. "A ghost followed us home."

"That's enough about ghosts," the man said. He took Kayo's arm and dragged her past the cart that was now half covered with dolls. He climbed the exit stairs, pulling Kayo with him.

The woman trailed after them. "What are you going to do with her?" she said.

"I'll think of something."

"We don't have a lookout now," the woman said.

"I know that," he snapped. "It's more important to keep this kid under control."

When they reached the second floor, Kayo saw that the thieves had a flashlight, the kind Rosie's parents bought for their motorhome. The flashlight sat on the floor, throwing light across the displays of dolls and toys.

Several of the glass display cases stood open, their contents gone.

"Get the rest of the good ones," the man said to the woman.

She put a key into the lock on the display case containing dolls of Little Red Riding-Hood and the Wolf, and Goldilocks and the Three Bears. She opened the case.

Kayo looked toward the display case that held

the musical cat. It remained locked. She wondered what would happen if the woman opened that case.

Would the crying ghost of the little girl appear to claim her toy? Would Werner von Moltz come?

If I can get the ghosts to come, Kayo thought, they might scare the thieves away.

Chapter

10

You're leaving behind the most valuable toy in the whole collection," Kayo said.

"What?" the man said. "Which one?"

Kayo pointed. "The musical cat."

The woman walked quickly to the display case and looked at the cat. "Not true," she said. "It's a nice little toy and it's in good condition, but it won't bring nearly as much as the dolls we're taking."

"It will if you know its history," Kayo said. "That cat belonged to King George of England when he was a little boy."

Kayo had no idea who had ruled Great Britain at the time the musical cat was made, but she thought there had been a King George at one time.

"This kid should be writing fiction," the man

said. "First ghosts and now the King of England. Gimme a break."

"If the toy had a royal background," the woman said, "you can be sure the museum would advertise that fact." She turned away from the cat's display case.

I went too far, Kayo thought. I'll have to be careful what I tell them or they may not believe anything I say.

The woman lifted Goldilocks out of the case.

"My mother is coming to pick me up soon," Kayo said. "If I'm not waiting for her by the front door, she will call the police."

Maybe Mom *will* come, Kayo thought. Rosie and I are supposed to be on the bus that gets home at 5:45. When we aren't on it Mom will worry that something is wrong. She'll try to find us.

"I'm going to start loading the van," the woman said. "It's too risky to stay here."

"The ghost that followed us was a German soldier," Kayo said. "He was killed in World War I."

The woman dropped Goldilocks. She turned to look at Kayo. "My great-grandfather died in World War I," the woman said. "When my grandmother saw his ghost, he was wearing his uniform."

"This ghost wore a uniform, too," Kayo said, "and a helmet. There was a blue light all around him, and even after he disappeared, we smelled a damp musty smell where he stood."

The woman gazed at Kayo, her eyes wide. "She's telling the truth, Dutch," she said. "I know she is. She couldn't make up a story like that."

"The ghost followed my friend and me home from the museum," Kayo said. "Last night he appeared in my bedroom in the middle of the night."

"Just like Grandma," the woman said.

"That does it!" the man said. "I don't care if the ghost of Christopher Columbus follows us home. We have a job to do here, and the longer we stand around talking, the greater the chance we'll get caught. So let's quit yakking and get on with it."

"What about the girl?" the woman asked. She picked up the doll she had dropped. Kayo was glad Goldilocks had landed on the carpet.

"We'll lock her in one of these empty cases," the man said. "She won't be able to call the cops from in there."

"There's still somebody in the bathroom, too."

"Let her stay there; she hasn't seen or heard anything. From the way she was screaming she's probably so scared she'll stay in there all night. By then we'll have our money from Tuttle and be on our way to Spokane."

"It's a ghost in the bathroom," Kayo said.

The woman hesitated for a moment, looking at Kayo, before she carried another armful of dolls down the stairs.

The man pulled Kayo to an empty display case next to the one that held the cat. The glass door stood open.

Kayo looked at the enclosure. All of the display cases were higher than the museum floor; most had large drawers below them which pulled out to display other exhibits. Kayo guessed that the case was four feet wide, four feet deep, and about five feet high. Kayo would fit inside the case, but there wouldn't be any room to spare. She would be able to sit down only if she drew her knees up to her chest.

He pulled out the drawer, to make a step. Two china baby dolls in white dresses lay in the drawer, their innocent eyes looking up at Kayo and the thief through a covering of thick glass.

"Climb in," he said.

There won't be enough air, Kayo thought. He might as well lock me in a glass coffin.

"In," the man repeated, shoving Kayo toward the drawer. His dark gloves felt warm on her shoulders. She caught a whiff of aftershave lotion blended with sweat, and her stomach turned over.

The man put his hands on Kayo's waist, lifted

her, and set her feet on top of the drawer. Then he shoved her into the display case. He pushed with such force that she hit her head on the back wall, stunning her long enough for him to close both the drawer and the glass door.

The woman rushed back up the stairs. "The phone rang while I was downstairs," she said, "and an answering device came on. The caller was a woman who said her daughter and a friend visited the museum this afternoon and failed to arrive home when they were supposed to. The woman said since there was no answer she assumed the girls had left. Unless someone from the museum calls right back, she is going to call the police and report them missing."

Yes! Kayo thought. Call the police, Mom. Now!

While the man held the door shut, he spoke over his shoulder to the woman. "Go downstairs and play that message back. Get the phone number and call the kid's mother. Make up a name; tell her you're from the museum. Say that the girls missed their bus and an employee is driving them home."

Listening to the man's instructions, Kayo clenched her fists in frustration. His plan would work. Even if Mom had already called the police, she would call them back and tell them they didn't have to look for two girls, after all, because someone from the museum was bringing them safely home. Mom would wait another hour before she would suspect that something was wrong, that no one from the doll museum was bringing the girls home. By then Kayo might be out of air.

"Give me the keys," the man said as he held out his hand. "And be sure to erase the message after you listen to it."

The woman nodded and tossed the ring of keys to the man before she hurried downstairs.

He made a one-handed grab for the keys and missed. They rattled to the floor. When he bent to pick them up, he moved away from the glass door for an instant.

Kayo shoved hard from the inside. The door opened far enough for her to squeeze one foot out.

The man tried to stuff Kayo's foot back inside the case. She leaned her shoulder into the door and pushed. The door jerked open, striking the man's collarbone.

He stumbled backward, accidentally stepping on the keys. His ankle twisted and he flailed his arms, trying to catch his balance.

Before he could slam the door shut again, Kayo jumped out of the display case.

The man grabbed her arm.

Kayo wrenched free, spun away, and sprinted

through the dark museum toward the rest room. If she could make it there, Rosie would let her in and they would both be safe.

Heavy footsteps pounded behind her.

He was close. Too close.

And he was getting closer.

Chapter

11

*R*osie paced nervously around the bathroom. She looked at her watch. Six-fifteen.

Why didn't Kayo come?

It's been too long, she thought. If Kayo made it to the telephone and called for help, the police would be here by now. As soon as they arrived Kayo would come to get me.

But Kayo had not come, nor had the police.

Something went wrong, Rosie decided. Kayo never made the call. The thieves must have caught her. If so, where was she now? Were the thieves still in the museum? Had they tied Kayo up and left? Had they taken Kayo with them?

Rosie turned off the bathroom light. She couldn't wait any longer, not when Kayo might need help.

Rosie unlocked the bathroom door and cracked it open. Putting an ear to the opening, she listened. She heard voices somewhere in the museum, but she could not make out who it was or what they were saying.

Rosie opened the door and slipped out, easing the door shut so it wouldn't make any noise.

The museum was still dark. Rosie's heart beat faster. If the police had come they would have turned the lights on. The voices must be the man and woman in ski masks.

It sounded as if they were on the second floor. Rosie moved slowly through the dark museum toward the voices. Although her eyes adjusted to the darkness, she held her hands out in front of her as she walked, fearful that she would bump into something and make a noise again. Each time she came to the end of a corridor, she peeked around the corner before she continued into the next display area.

She was getting close to the voices when her hands hit glass. Rosie stopped. It was the door of a display case, standing open. The case was empty. She came to other empty display cases where the thieves had removed the dolls.

Anger surged through Rosie. Those thieves were not only stealing from the museum owner, they were robbing all of the people who liked to come and enjoy the collection. It wasn't right.

"Rosie!" Kayo's cry jolted Rosie, setting every nerve on edge. "Unlock the door!"

She's running from the thieves, Rosie realized. She's headed this way, toward the rest room, and I'm not there.

"You won't make it!" the man shouted, and Rosie knew instantly that his voice was too close. She could not get back to the rest room before he saw her.

Instead of running she climbed into an empty display case and pulled the door shut. She smiled and held her arms out, waist high, spreading her fingers. She stood absolutely still, barely breathing.

There are some life-size dolls, she thought. I might get away with this.

Kayo ran past the stuffed horse pulling a wagon load of dolls. She ran past the doll hospital.

When she rounded the corner the man was only a few feet behind her. Kayo was fast but so was the man, and with his long legs he gained on her with every step.

Rosie saw them coming. Run, Kayo! she thought. Run fast! The bathroom door is unlocked.

Just as Kayo passed the case where Rosie was, the man leaped forward and tackled her. His hands closed around her ankles.

Rosie watched, horrified, as Kayo fell.

Rosie wanted to jump out of the case and attack the man, but she knew it was better to stand where she was, with her smile frozen on her face and her unmoving hands in the air. If he didn't realize she was there, she might be able to sneak downstairs and get to the telephone. It was smarter to call for help than to fight with the thief.

The man stood up, pulling Kayo to her feet. Holding her by both shoulders, he pushed her in front of him, out of Rosie's sight. As soon as they were gone, Rosie climbed out of the case and tiptoed back toward the stairway.

The man pushed Kayo to where the keys lay on the floor. Still holding on to Kayo, he picked up the keys. Then he pulled out the drawer, lifted Kayo onto it, and shoved her inside the empty case.

He leaned his body against the door while he tried to insert a key in the keyhole. It didn't fit. He tried a different key. It wouldn't work, either.

On the third try the key slid smoothly into the keyhole. Kayo heard the *click* as the door locked.

The woman returned. "I talked to the mother," she said. "I told her I was driving the girls home, and she believed me."

Rosie passed the rest room, wishing she could go back inside, lock the door, and wait until help arrived, even if nobody came until morning.

If she were alone with the thieves, that is what she would do. But she couldn't think only of her own safety; she had to think of Kayo, as well. The man had seemed angry when he caught Kayo. Rosie had no idea where he had taken Kayo or what he planned to do. For all she knew the thieves were armed.

Tempting as it was to wait alone in the safe rest room, she could not do it.

Instead she made her way down the stairs, moving slowly and carefully. At the landing she sat down, the way Kayo had, and bumped down the rest of the steps.

The downstairs room was empty. She heard voices from upstairs again. Maybe she could call for help now, before they came down.

Rosie ran to the circular counter and felt for the doorknob. The door was locked.

She heard voices at the top of the exit stairs. The thieves were coming down.

Rosie ran to the far side of the counter and squatted down.

"I still say we should leave now," the woman said.

"One more cart load," the man said. "Then, if you're still jittery, we'll go and come back for the rest another night."

"No," the woman said. "I'm never coming

back. And if any ghosts follow us, I'm dumping the dolls."

The thieves reached the landing and continued down. Where is Kayo? Rosie wondered. What have they done with Kayo?

"I can't believe you let that kid scare you," the man said. "There are no such things as ghosts. She was making up stories, trying to frighten us, just like she lied when she said her mother was coming to pick her up. None of it was true." He began pulling the cart full of dolls away from the stairs.

"Maybe so," the woman said. "But the idea of seeing a ghost makes my hair stand on end."

Rosie hesitated for only a moment. If she hid and waited to call the police after the thieves had left, they would probably get away with all the dolls. She wanted to make them leave now, before they took the dolls out of the museum.

"Goooooo," Rosie said. She spoke softly with a waver in her voice, making the word sound like a moan. It was the way she had imagined a ghost would sound until she actually heard the ghost of Werner von Moltz speak.

The thieves stopped.

"What was that?" the woman said. "Who's there?"

Rosie moaned again, slightly louder. She cupped her hands around her mouth and tried to make it sound as if her voice came from the empty office. "Gooooo awaaayyy."

"It's the ghost," the woman said. "Dutch! The ghost is here."

"Don't be an idiot," the man said. "It's probably the second kid, trying to scare us."

"Goooo nowwwwww," moaned Rosie.

"You can do what you like with the dolls," the woman said. "I'm not staying where there are ghosts." She hurried down the hallway toward the elevator and the employee workroom.

Swearing, the man approached the counter, making no effort to be quiet. As he came around the counter one way, Rosie moved quickly the other way, bent at the waist.

The man suddenly reversed directions and sprinted around the counter.

Rosie could not respond fast enough.

"I knew it!" he cried as he spotted Rosie. "Darlene! Come back. There's no ghost; it's the other kid, just like I said."

The woman returned.

Rosie stood and faced the thieves. She could not see their faces through the ski masks, but she knew she would never forget their voices.

"Some ghost," the man said. He grabbed Rosie's arm. "Come on. Let's go visit your pal."

Rosie did not struggle. She knew she was not fast enough or strong enough to get away.

The Ghost Followed Us Home

"I've been thinking about the toy that belonged to King George," the man said to the woman as they climbed the stairs. "Maybe the kid knows something the museum isn't advertising. Her parents probably know the owner or she would not be in here at night. Maybe that really is the most valuable piece in the museum, but they don't want the public to know."

"Maybe they're afraid of theft," the woman said.

The man laughed.

"I'll go get it," the woman said.

He handed her a ring of keys.

Rosie tried to think which toy had belonged to King George, but she could not remember.

When they reached the second floor the woman kept going. The man stopped in front of the first empty display case, a freestanding square one. He gave Rosie a push.

"In you go," he said.

A chill of horror prickled Rosie's scalp.

He is going to lock me in there, she realized, and I won't have enough air.

Thump. Thump. Thump.

The noise came from around the corner, in the next corridor where the musical cat was. It's the ghost girl, Rosie thought. She's there, pounding on the glass.

Rosie expected the woman to come running

back. She had seemed genuinely afraid of ghosts, and she must hear the noise.

"Get in," the man said.

Thump. Thump. Thump.

"Do you hear that?" Rosie said. "That's one of the ghosts. She wants us to open the case she's in."

"And I'm head coach of the San Diego Chargers," the man said.

Thump. Thump. Thump.

"It is a ghost," Rosie said. "I'll prove it to you. Come on." She walked around the corner toward the thumping noise.

Chuckling, the man followed.

Rosie started toward the musical cat and then stopped when she realized the thumping came from a display case on the other side of the cat. She looked toward the noise.

"Oh, no!" she gasped. It wasn't the ghost girl pounding on the glass. It was Kayo.

Thump! Thump! Kayo beat her fists on the inside of the door, looking angry and scared and helpless.

"Let her out of there!" Rosie demanded.

"Anything else you want to show me?" the man said.

Chapter

12

The man reached for Rosie's arm.

Rosie twisted away from him and ran. Fear put speed in her feet; she sprinted around the corner and toward the stairs.

He caught her before she could start down. He pulled her to the corridor where the woman was and pushed her to an empty case near the one Kayo was in.

Rosie remembered the doll that had been in that case. It was a French doll with a beautiful long dress. Rosie had always liked the doll's ringlets and the wreath on her hair. They took it, she thought, and they're going to get away with it.

"Get in," he said. "Now."

"No."

He raised his hand as if to strike her.

Rosie swallowed her anger and climbed into the case. Tears stung her eyes as she wondered what would happen now. She knew Mrs. Benton would call Rosie's parents when the girls did not arrive.

Mom and Dad would look for her and Kayo. Mrs. Benton would look for them. Before long, the police would look for them. Probably whole search parties would look for them.

But would anyone look in the doll museum? Rosie worried that everyone would assume something happened to the girls on their way home. No one would think to look for them here.

We'll be found tomorrow morning, Rosie thought, when the museum opens. But will we still be alive?

Kayo watched as the woman put a key into the lock on the display case that contained the musical cat. Yes, she thought. Open that one.

Kayo waited holding her breath. She was certain that Chantal, the ghost girl, would appear as soon as the door opened.

Kayo hoped both ghosts came to get the cat. She wanted the ghosts to appear right in that awful woman's face and scare her out of her wits.

The woman turned the key.

The door swung open.

The Ghost Followed Us Home

"Chantal!" Kayo cried. "The case is open. Come and get your cat!"

Nothing happened.

There was no sign of the weeping child.

Kayo's shoulders sagged. What a joke, she thought. I lay awake half of last night fearing a ghost would come, and now I'm disappointed because a ghost didn't come.

The woman reached in and picked up the mohair cat.

Me and my big mouth, Kayo thought. They did not plan to steal the musical cat until I made up that stupid story about King George. Now the thieves think the cat is worth a ton of money. Thanks to me our favorite toy is going to be sold to some collector overseas. We'll never see it again, and neither will any of the people who visit the doll museum in the future.

Why didn't I tell them it was the big doll in the same case with the cat, the one sitting in a chair, that was valuable? Or I could have said the oil lamp in that case belonged to King George. All I wanted was for them to unlock that door. Why did I mention the cat at all?

She watched as the woman examined the cat, turning it over in her hands.

Maybe the ghosts are waiting until the cat is outside, Kayo thought. Maybe the German soldier and the crying ghost girl will follow the thieves and take the cat later, when there are no more doors to get through.

She hoped so. If the musical cat could not stay here in the museum, Kayo wanted it to go to France, to make little Chantal happy and to ease Werner von Moltz's guilt. She wanted both ghosts to find peace.

The woman carried the cat past Kayo's case. Kayo pushed on the glass again even though she knew it was hopeless. The woman did not look at her.

The air was already stuffy inside the case. Kayo pressed her warm forehead against the smooth, cold glass.

If she wasn't found quickly, she feared she would be a ghost soon herself. And Rosie, too.

The man stood in front of Rosie's door, holding it closed.

The woman tucked the cat under her arm. She handed the keys to the man so he could lock the case that Rosie was in.

He inserted the key in the keyhole, but before he turned it, the woman screamed.

Her shrill cry bounced off the glass display cases.

The man spun around to see what was wrong.

The woman fainted, crumpling to the floor at his feet.

The musical cat did not fall with her. It remained suspended in the air as if supported by invisible hands.

"What?" The man backed away from the cat, leaving the keys dangling from the door of the display case.

The sides of the cat began to move in and out. The strange music filled the air.

The man knelt and shook the woman. "Wake up!" he said. "We're leaving."

The woman remained motionless.

So did Rosie. She was afraid if she moved or made a sound, the man would realize he had never locked the door. Standing as still as one of the dolls, she watched the man gather the woman in his arms and carry her toward the stairway.

The musical cat continued its song.

As soon as the thieves turned the corner, Rosie pushed on the door of her case. The door swung open, and Rosie climbed out.

She pulled the keys from the lock and ran to the display case where Kayo was.

She tried keys until she found the right one. When the door opened, Kayo jumped to the floor.

Neither girl spoke. Holding hands, they walked to the top of the exit stairway and looked down. The man was halfway down the steps, still carrying the woman.

The music stopped.

The thieves reached the bottom of the stairs.

When they got to the cart full of dolls, the man lowered the woman's feet until they touched the floor. Supporting her under her arms, he shook her again. "Wake up," he said. "You have to walk while I pull the cart."

The woman blinked and swayed. "I saw a ghost," she said. "Did you see her, Dutch? Did you see the ghost?"

"Calm down," the man said.

"Where is she?" the woman said. "Where is the ghost now?"

"There isn't any ghost."

"You didn't see the little girl? She had on an old-fashioned dress and an apron, and she took that mohair cat out of my hands and started playing music with it. She was right there in front of us. You must have seen her."

"Well, I didn't," he said. He grabbed the cart handle and pulled it toward the hallway.

The woman staggered after him.

The cart squeaked louder now that it was loaded with dolls. The woman continued to talk about the ghost while the man insisted she had imagined it.

Kayo and Rosie crept down the stairs and hurried to the front door.

Rosie turned the handle. As she pushed the door open, Kayo tapped her on the shoulder. Rosie looked back.

Chantal's ghost floated toward the door, carrying the musical cat.

Rosie and Kayo glanced at each other, nodded agreement, and pushed the door open wide. Standing together they held it open and waited for the ghost.

Chantal cradled the cat close to her chest as if it were a baby. She paused at the threshold and smiled at Rosie and Kayo. Her face shone with happiness.

"*Merci,*" Chantal said.

"You're welcome," Rosie whispered.

The girls felt a gentle, cool breeze when the ghost passed them. A faint scent of fresh hay lingered after her.

Rosie and Kayo watched as Chantal Dubail and her musical cat drifted across the museum steps, floated high above the parking lot, and disappeared into the night sky.

Rosie started to close the door, but Kayo stopped her. She pointed to the left. A large van was parked close to the building, far in the corner.

"There must be a back door," Kayo whispered. "Let's go in and call the police. They might get here while the thieves are loading their van."

The girls went inside. The cart's squeak came from far down the hallway.

While Rosie carefully closed the front door,

Kayo climbed over the counter. She found the telephone and dialed 911.

"We need help," Kayo whispered. "At the doll museum."

Rosie looked over the counter. Kayo motioned for her to come. Rosie climbed over the counter and sat on the floor next to Kayo.

"The emergency operator said the police would be here in a couple of minutes," Kayo whispered. "It's probably safer to wait here than to go outside."

The squeaking stopped.

Rosie and Kayo listened.

"The door to the workroom is locked," the man said.

"It can't be," the woman said. "We left it open in case we needed to get out fast."

"Somebody locked it, and I can't open it without the key."

"It was those girls," the woman said. "Those girls must have locked the door."

Kayo and Rosie smiled at each other in the dim light. They had a good idea who had locked the door. It was the same person who had locked the bathroom door yesterday so that Rosie and Kayo would have to stay in the museum when everyone else was gone. Werner von Moltz.

"Give me the keys," the man said.

The Ghost Followed Us Home

"I don't have the keys," the woman said. "You have them."

"No, I don't."

"I gave them to you so you could lock up the second girl."

"I left them in the lock," he said. "I'll go get them."

"I'll come with you. I'm not staying here alone. The ghost might come back."

The voices came closer. The thieves were walking fast.

We should have run when we had the chance, Rosie thought. By now we would be a block away instead of huddled here, hoping the thieves don't look over the counter.

"There was no ghost, I tell you. Look around. Do you see any ghost? Do you hear any music? No. Of course not. Because you imagined the whole thing. You let those kids and their wild stories get to you."

"What if she follows us?" the woman said. "If that ghost appears in my bedroom tonight, I'll have a heart attack."

The voices were entering the reception area.

"Maybe we can get out this door," the woman said.

"The van is next to the back door. And we have to load the dolls. I'll run up and get the keys."

"We could move the van and take the dolls out this way."

"Sure we could. And every car that drives past would see us. Why not just put out a sign: Burglary in Progress?"

"I am never setting foot in this place again," the woman said.

Rosie and Kayo heard heavy footsteps clomp across the floor and go up the stairs.

"They're gone!" the man yelled from above. The footsteps pounded back down.

"The kids are gone, and so are the keys." His voice shook with fury. "They got away and took our keys with them."

"They're probably hiding in the bathroom," the woman said.

"I'm going to disconnect the telephone," he said. "We need time to load the van. I don't want them to sneak in here and call for help."

Putting both hands on the countertop, he vaulted over.

When he landed, he looked down.

"Look who's here," he said. "A pair of ghosts."

Chapter

13

The girls stood up, facing the man.

"Give me the keys," he said.

"We don't have them," Rosie said.

"The ghost took them," Kayo said.

"You two have spoiled a perfect job," the man said, "and now you're going to wish you hadn't."

"We called the police," Kayo said. "They are on the way."

"More lies," the man muttered. His hands, in the black gloves, reached toward Rosie.

"Help!" Kayo shouted. "Werner! We need help!"

As Kayo called his name she wondered whether the ghost was still there. Now that Chantal had left with her toy, there was no reason for Werner von Moltz to stay at the museum. By now he might already be in France with Chantal. Or back in Germany. Or even at peace so he didn't appear as a ghost any longer.

The gloved hands closed on Rosie's arms.

"Werner!" Rosie cried. "Help!"

A blue glow lit the room behind the girls. Rosie and Kayo could smell the musty odor.

The man's hands stopped.

"Dutch!" The woman's voice vibrated with fear. "Look!"

The blue light grew brighter.

The man dropped his hands and took a step backward, away from the girls.

The woman screamed.

The man turned and climbed over the counter. He and the woman ran together toward the front door.

Werner von Moltz, in his uniform and helmet, appeared in front of them. He held one hand up.

"Halt!" he commanded.

The woman slumped to the floor.

The man tried to walk around the ghost.

"Halt!" Werner von Moltz repeated.

The man stopped. "Who—who are you?" he said.

Sirens screamed in the street.

The thief turned toward the hallway, but Werner von Moltz again blocked his way.

The thief made a fist and swung at the ghost.

His fist went straight through the ghost and out the other side. Werner von Moltz did not flinch.

The thief pulled his hand back and looked at it as if he had never seen fingers before.

"They are not yours," the ghost said.

The thief stared at the ghost, his mouth open. "What?" he said. "What do you want?"

"The dolls are not yours. They are loyal childhood friends and they must stay here, where those who loved them can visit and remember."

Red lights whirled in the dark outside as two police cars pulled into the museum parking lot. The sirens stopped.

The spinning red lights shone through the glass door from outside, blending with the blue glow inside.

It's like a crazy laser video, Kayo thought.

Bright flashlights came on in the parking lot, pointed at the door.

The ghost vanished.

The woman moaned and sat up. "It's all over, Dutch," she said.

"No!" he cried. "We can still get away. Run!" He turned and dashed down the dark hallway toward the locked door.

The woman got to her feet.

Rosie and Kayo heard the man kicking at the door, trying to force it open.

As the girls climbed over the counter, they heard the sound of wood splintering.

The woman started groggily toward the hallway, but Kayo grabbed the back of her ski mask and held tight.

"Dutch!" the woman yelled. "Help! The ghost caught me!"

Two police officers ran up the museum steps. Rosie opened the door.

Officer Ken Bremner and Officer Julia Harig rushed into the museum.

Rosie pointed down the hallway. "That way," she said. "He's trying to get out the back door."

Officer Bremner ran down the hallway.

"This is his partner," Kayo said, letting go of the woman's ski mask. "They tried to steal the dolls."

"They locked us in the empty display cases," Rosie said.

The woman in the ski mask leaned against the reception counter.

"Are you Kayo Benton and Rosie Saunders?" Officer Harig asked. When the girls said yes, she said, "Call your parents. They reported you missing about half an hour ago. They are plenty worried about you."

Kayo reached over and lifted the telephone on to the counter. She called her mother, and Rosie called her parents.

Another police car arrived and two more officers came in. A woman ran up the steps behind them and started to follow them in the door.

"Sorry. No admittance," an officer said.

"I'm Lauren Verrilli," the woman said. "I'm a docent at the museum." Rosie and Kayo recognized her as the woman who had been at the reception counter the day before.

"Let her in," Officer Harig said.

Lauren entered. "I live across the street," she said, "and I saw the police cars. What happened? Did someone break in?"

"Can you turn the lights on?" Officer Harig said.

Lauren went into the small office, and seconds later the museum lights blazed on.

Rosie and Kayo listened as Officer Harig read the woman in the ski mask her rights.

"There are ghosts here," the woman said. "I saw them. One was a little girl and one was a soldier. They played music on the toy cat."

"Better order some mental tests on her," one of the officers said.

Officer Bremner returned with the other thief.

"There's a cart full of dolls at the end of the hall," Officer Bremner said. "Looks as if they planned to go through the workroom and out the fire-escape door to their van."

Lauren ran to get the cart.

"Tell them, Dutch," the woman said. "Tell them we really saw ghosts."

"I didn't see any ghost," the man said.

Rosie reached in her jeans pocket. "Here's a set of museum keys," she said.

Officer Bremner looked hard at Rosie and Kayo as he took the keys. "Aren't you the same girls who caught the vandals at the school?" he asked.

"Yes," Kayo said.

"And you found the poisonous plant in that old woman's yard."

"Mrs. Tallie," Rosie said.

"That's the one," he said.

"Maybe we ought to sign them up for the police force," Officer Harig said. "They solve half the crimes in Oakwood before we do."

Lauren Verrilli put the dolls and toys away while Rosie and Kayo told the police what had happened. Neither girl mentioned the ghosts. It seemed better, somehow, just to tell about the thieves and leave Chantal Dubail and Werner von Moltz out of the story.

Part way through, Mr. and Mrs. Saunders drove in to the parking lot. Mrs. Benton was with them. Rosie and Kayo started over and told everything again.

They had just finished answering questions from the police when Lauren came downstairs.

"There's only one item missing from the upper

level exhibits," she said. "It's a musical cat, made in France. It wasn't on the cart and it isn't in any of the display cases."

"The ghost took it," the woman said. "I've been trying to tell you that."

"Let's get her to the hospital," Officer Harig said.

"Dutch!" the woman said. "Tell them what happened. You saw the second ghost, too. I know you did."

"I don't believe in ghosts," the man said.

Officer Bremner clamped handcuffs on the man's wrists and led him to the patrol car. Officer Harig followed with the woman.

"They must have hidden the cat," another officer said. "We didn't find anything in their van except some reference books with the current prices of antique dolls."

"I wonder why they took that one item?" Lauren said. "It isn't nearly as valuable as many of the others."

Kayo and Rosie smiled at each other and said nothing.

Chapter
14

"It was you, wasn't it?" Sammy Hulenback demanded the next day, when Rosie and Kayo got to school. "You caught the thieves at the doll museum."

"What can he be talking about?" Rosie said.

"I have no idea," Kayo replied.

"I heard all about it on the radio this morning," Sammy said. "You caught the thieves and called the police."

"Were our names mentioned?" Kayo asked. She knew they were not, because Rosie's parents always insisted that the girls' names not be used in any news report.

"No," Sammy admitted, "but as soon as the reporter said the doll museum, I knew right away it was you. You didn't have operations on your big toes yesterday. You went after the thieves."

"Maybe we did and maybe we didn't," Kayo said.

"Your club goofed this time," Sammy said.

"The thieves are in jail, aren't they?" Rosie said.

"Ha!" Sammy cried. "It was you! I knew it."

The girls walked toward their sixth-grade classroom. Sammy followed.

"You goofed," he said, "because one toy is still missing. It said on the radio that the thieves hid a musical cat somewhere and the police can't find it."

"Don't believe everything you hear on the radio," Kayo said.

"Do you know where the cat is?" Sammy asked.

The girls did not answer.

"You probably kept it yourselves," Sammy asked.

"Strike one," Kayo said.

"You did! You're so crazy about animals, you stole the toy cat yourself and you're letting the thieves take the blame."

"Strike two," Kayo said.

"The radio said the cat was really old," Sammy said.

"It was made circa 1900," Rosie said. She took

out her vocabulary notebook and made a check mark.

"If you were going to steal a toy cat," Sammy said, "why wouldn't you take a new one?"

"Strike three," Kayo said. "You are out of this conversation."

The girls sat in adjoining desks in the front row. Sammy, who always sat in the last row, stood beside them for a moment. "I heard the dolls that were nearly stolen are worth six hundred thousand dollars," he said.

"That's right," Kayo said.

"Do you want to go to the doll museum with me after school today?" Sammy asked.

"We can't," Kayo said. "We're picking up information about Greyhound Rescue, for a school report."

"We probably aren't going back to the museum for a long time," Rosie said.

"I'm going today after school," Sammy said. "I'll look around for that musical cat. If I find it, will you let me in your club?"

"You won't find it," Kayo said.

"How do you know? The thieves might have tossed it into the bushes."

"The cat is not in the bushes," Rosie said.

"Where is it then?" He squinted at Rosie as if he could see inside her head and read the answer to his question. "You know where it is, don't you?"

Rosie motioned for Sammy to lean down so she could whisper in his ear. "The cat is in France."

"You're lying," Sammy said. "How would it get to France? You lied about your big toes and you lied about going to the circus at midnight, and now you're lying about the cat." He stomped back to his own seat.

"Circus?" Kayo said. "What circus?"

Rosie was laughing so hard she could hardly answer. "When he asked what time we would get home yesterday, I told him *circa* midnight. He thought . . ." Both girls gave in to a fit of giggles.

When they finally quit laughing, Rosie said, "Do you realize we had an adventure that was not an official Care Club project?"

"It may not have been official," Kayo said, "but we did help an animal get returned to its home." She smiled at Rosie. "A toy animal."

"Chantal looked so happy last night," Rosie said. "Maybe we should add a line to the Care Club charter, vowing to help all ghosts."

"I do not plan to meet another ghost," Kayo said.

"I'm glad we met the ones we did, though. I wonder if Werner von Moltz will bring the cat back after Chantal doesn't need it anymore."

"He'll try."

"It's odd, isn't it?" Rosie said. "That first night, when he appeared in your house, we were terrified. Now we think of him as a friend. I kind of hope we'll see him again."

"We were scared of the unknown," Kayo said. "Once we understood the ghosts and their problems, there was no reason to be afraid."

"The only thing I'm afraid of now," Rosie said, "is that Sammy will keep bugging us to let him join Care Club."

OAKWOOD DAILY HERALD   Sunday Edition

MUSEUM'S TOY CAT FOUND IN FRANCE

A musical cat which was stolen from the Oakwood Doll Museum is being returned to the museum, but its return is as much a mystery as its theft.

A clerk at the American embassy in Paris found the mohair cat this morning on the desk of the American ambassador to France.

Neither the clerk nor the ambassador could explain how the toy got into the embassy during the night. Nothing in the building, where night security guards were on duty, had been disturbed or removed.

The Ghost Followed Us Home

The musical cat, which was made in France circa 1900, was stolen from the doll museum last Wednesday night. No one at the museum knew how the toy got to France.

"We thought the thieves hid it around here," said Lauren Verrilli, the museum docent who cataloged the items that had been removed from their cases during the break-in.

According to Police Officer Julia Harig, two people were arrested for attempted burglary and for assault on the girls who discovered them in the museum. The alleged burglars remain in the county jail.

The American ambassador to France called Oakwood police because an anonymous note with the cat asked that it be sent to the Oakwood Doll Museum.

The note was written in German.

On Monday morning Kayo said, "I used up my film yesterday, and Mom said she would drop it at Fine Fotos on her way to work. My pictures will be ready this afternoon."

"Let's go get them after school."

When the girls picked up the prints, they flipped quickly through photos of Homer and Diamond, Mrs. Benton's birthday cake, and Kayo's baseball team.

They both wanted to see the one picture that was taken late at night in Kayo's bedroom.

When they found it they held it between them and stared.

The picture had a faint blue tinge as if the developer had made a mistake.

It showed Rosie's bedroom door, with the Willie Mays poster.

It showed part of Homer, with his back humped high and his tail huge.

And, barely visible, it showed a German soldier in a World War I uniform.

Author's Notes

All of the dolls and toys described in *The Ghost Followed Us Home*, including the musical cat, are currently on display at the Rosalie Whyel Museum of Doll Art in Bellevue, Washington, recipient of the Jumeau Trophy for The Best Private Doll Museum World Wide.

I am grateful to Rosalie Whyel for her help and cooperation. She answered questions, offered assistance, allowed me to describe her beautiful facility, shared photographs, and even took the musical cat out of its case so I could touch it and listen to its song.

The cat's World War I history came from my imagination. Chantal Dubail and Werner von Moltz are fictional characters, and so are their ghosts.

*   *   *

FRIGHTMARES

There are several nonprofit organizations whose sole purpose is to find homes for ex-racing greyhounds. For more information, contact the Greyhound Adoption Network, 1–800–G–HOUNDS. You will be referred to the adoption group nearest you.

About the Author

Peg Kehret's popular novels for young people are regularly nominated for state awards. She has received the Young Hoosier Award, the Golden Sower Award, the Iowa Children's Choice Award, the Celebrate Literacy Award, the Sequoyah Award, the Land of Enchantment Award, the Maud Hart Lovelace Award, and the Pacific Northwest Young Reader's Choice Award. She lives with her husband, Carl, and their animal friends in Washington State, where she is a volunteer at the Humane Society and SPCA. Her two grown children and four grandchildren live in Washington, too.

Peg's Minstrel titles include *Nightmare Mountain; Sisters, Long Ago; Cages; Terror at the Zoo; Horror at the Haunted House;* and the *Frightmares*™ series.

Don't miss any of the adventure!

FRIGHTMARES™

Whenever pets–and their owners–get into trouble, Rosie Saunders
and Kayo Benton always seem to be in the middle of the action.
Ever since they started the Care Club ("We Care About Animals"),
they've discovered a world of mysteries and surprises. . .and danger!

#1: CAT BURGLAR ON THE PROWL
#2: BONE BREATH AND THE VANDALS
#3: DON'T GO NEAR MRS. TALLIE
#4: DESERT DANGER
#5: THE GHOST FOLLOWED US HOME

By Peg Kehret

A MINSTREL® BOOK

Published by Pocket Books   1049-05

Bruce Coville's Alien Adventures

What happens when a tiny spaceship crashes through Rod Allbright's window and drops a crew of superpowerful aliens into the middle of his school project? Rod is drafted by Captain Grakker to help the aliens catch a dangerous interstellar criminal–in a chase that takes them all over the galaxy!

ALIENS ATE MY HOMEWORK
I LEFT MY SNEAKERS IN DIMENSION X
THE SEARCH FOR SNOUT

by BRUCE COVILLE

A MINSTREL® BOOK

Published by Pocket Books   1043-03